My First Book of
SOUNDS

formerly titled *Bow Wow! Meow! A First Book of*

By Melanie Bellah
Pictures by Trina Schart

A Golden Book • New York
Western Publishing Company, Inc., Racine, Wisconsin 53404

What does the kitty say?
Meow.

What does the doggie say?
Bow-wow.

What does the cow say?
Moooo.

What does the rooster say?
Cock-a-doodle-doo.

What sound does a car horn make?
Beep-beep.

What do the chicks say?
Peep-peep.

What does a siren sound like?
Oo-ooh, oo-ooh.

What sound does a train make?
Choo-choo-choo.

What does the duck say?
Quack, quack.

What noise does
a trolley make?
Click-clack,
click-clack.

What do the pigeons say?
Coo, coo.

What does the owl say?
Whoo.

What does the lamb say?
Baa, baa.

Who's that laughing?
Ha-ha-ha.

What sound does a bell make?
Ding-dong-ding.

What sound does a phone make?
Ting-a-ling-a-ling.

What does the horse say?
Neigh-hh.

What do the children say?
Hurray!

What does the bee say?
Bzzz.

What does the snake say?
Ssss.

What sound does the rain make?
Pitter-patter.

What does the monkey say?
Chatter-chatter.

What sound does the clock make?
Tick-tock, tick-tock.

Someone's at the door—
Knock, knock.

A baby is crying,
Boo-hoo-hoo.

A baby is playing,
Peekaboo.

How does the music sound?
La-la-la.

What does the doll say?
Mama.

What sound does
the wind make?
Whhh.

Let's be quiet:
Shhh.